Alma Flor Ada

F. Isabel Campoy

Translated by **Joe Hayes and Sharon Franco**

Celebrate
St. Patrick's Day
with Samantha and Lola

Illustrated by **Sandra Lavandeira**

ALFAGUARA

Samantha loves Irish dancing.
She likes to dress up and dance.
Wearing her pretty costume,
she joins in at every chance.
Lola admires her.
She would like to dance too!

"Look," says Lola as she skips around,
"I learned a few steps."

Her brother says, "With just three steps,
you've only begun."

Lola laughs, "One step at a time,
Tomás, is how the goal is won."

At school there will be a talent show
celebrating St. Patrick's Day,
with songs, dancing, music,
and a very funny play.

Samantha practices.
She likes to dance.
One, two, three…
Lola imitates her.
One, two, three…

Four, five, six.
This dance is so much fun!
One step at a time
is how the goal is won.

"Your shoes are so pretty.
What a fancy dress!
Your wig is so neat,
and curly hair is the best!"

"If you like them so much, you can try them too.
Go ahead, put them on.
They'll look great on you!"

11

"What's this noise?
What's all this jumping?" asks
Samantha's sister Victoria.
"What are you doing?"

"I learned a few steps," Lola says
as she skips around.
"Seven, eight, nine, ten."

Victoria says, "With just ten steps,
you've only begun."

Samantha laughs, "One step at a time,
Victoria, is how the goal is won."

13

For a St. Patrick's Day surprise
Samantha gives Lola a chance.

"Your name is on the program!
You're doing a solo dance."

"Me?" cries Lola nervously.
"I just know a few steps. I've only begun!"

"Remember, Lola, one step at a time
is how the goal is won."

What is St. Patrick's Day?

Saint Patrick was born in England, but he lived in Ireland for many years. England and Ireland are both countries in Europe.

Saint Patrick was a great person. He helped many people and was always generous to those in need. For this reason, he is considered a "saint" in the Catholic religion. Saint Patrick is the "patron saint" of the Irish people, which means he is their most important saint.

In the United States there are many Irish people whose ancestors arrived many, many years ago. They brought with them the custom of celebrating their saint's day. Today, St. Patrick's Day is celebrated with parades and parties in more than 100 cities in the United States!

One of the biggest, most colorful St. Patrick's Day parades takes place in New York City. They say that Irish soldiers held the first St. Patrick's Day parade in New York. That was many years ago, in 1762.

St. Patrick's Day is always celebrated on the day he died, March 17th. St. Patrick's Day is a religious holiday, but it is actually more than that. It is also a chance to celebrate Irish culture.

People dress in green to remember the color of the Irish countryside. Traditional Irish dances and the music of bagpipes make the parades lively. The bagpipe is a traditional Irish instrument.

In March, stores, schools, and houses are filled with Irish decorations, like the shamrock. This is a plant that grows all over Ireland.

The first Irish people believed that shamrocks could bring good luck. This belief is still common, not only in Ireland but in many other countries too.

Another Irish symbol that is often seen around St. Patrick's Day is the leprechaun. There are many legends about these fantastic little people.

They say that leprechauns are mischievous little elves who work as shoemakers. Each leprechaun keeps a hidden treasure at the end of the rainbow. The treasure is a big pot full of gold coins. To find it, you have to catch the leprechaun or simply make friends with him.

In every country where Catholic people live, they celebrate their patron saint. All these celebrations are as fun and interesting as St. Patrick's Day.

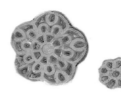

Boston College students ride a parade float through the streets of South Boston, Massachusetts on Saint Patrick's Day.
© Ted Spiegel/CORBIS

A man from Chicago, Illinois dressed to celebrate Saint Patrick's Day.
© Sandy Feisenthal/CORBIS

A group of girls watch the Saint Patrick's Day Parade in New York City.
© Catherine Leuthold/CORBIS

A big stuffed leprechaun blends in with the spectators of the Saint Patrick's Day Parade on Fifth Avenue in New York City.
© Joseph Sohm; ChromoSohm Inc./CORBIS

A man rides a miniature car in the Saint Patrick's Day Parade in San Diego, California.
© Richard Cummins/CORBIS

Participants in the Saint Patrick's Day Parade in New Orleans, Louisiana, throw necklaces from a float.
© Philip Gould/CORBIS

Two friends wear original costumes in the Saint Patrick's Day Parade in San Diego, California.
© Richard Cummins/CORBIS

Children wearing costumes in Las Fallas Procession in Valencia, Spain, celebrated in honor of the city's patron saint, Saint Joseph.
© Paul Almasy/CORBIS

The Chicago River is dyed green in celebration of Saint Patrick's Day in Chicago, Illinois.
© Sandy Feisenthal/CORBIS

Statues of Saint Felix and other saints carried through the streets of Vilafranca del Penedes, Spain.
© Stephanie Maze/CORBIS

Japanese bagpipers participate in the Saint Patrick's Day Parade in New York City.
© Szenes Jason/CORBIS SYGMA

A fleet of small boats accompany an image of Saint Nicholas, patron saint of travelers, during the festival in his honor in Bari, Italy.
© Fabian Ceballos/CORBIS SYGMA

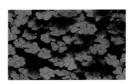
The shamrock is a symbol of Irish culture.
© Royalty-Free/CORBIS

Girls in Spanish dresses parade with small altars in the celebration of the Holy Child in Mandaue, Cebu, Philippines.
© Paul A. Souders/CORBIS

A boy with dyed green hair and a shamrock painted on his cheek participates in the Saint Patrick's Day Parade in San Diego, California.
© Richard Cummins/CORBIS

A juggler entertains hundreds of pilgrims who arrive to visit the Basilica of the Virgin of Guadalupe in Mexico City during the celebration in honor of the patron saint of Mexicans.
© Danny Lehman/CORBIS

Two friends wearing Irish hats participate in the Saint Patrick's Day Parade in Dover, Delaware.
© Kevin Fleming/CORBIS

Celebrate and Grow

Throughout history, and in all parts of the world, people get together to celebrate historic anniversaries, commemorate an important person's life, or to ring in a special period of the year. Common to all these celebrations is the acknowledgment that life is a marvelous gift, and that getting together with family and friends makes us happy.

In a multicultural society like that found in the United States, the fact that so many diverse groups live so closely together invites us to know our own culture better, and to discover the cultures of others. Anyone who explores his or her own culture recognizes his or her own identity in the mirror, and affirms his or her sense of belonging to a group. By learning about different cultures, we can observe life as it appears through the windows of those cultures.

This series offers children the opportunity to get closer to the rich cultural landscape of our communities.

St. Patrick's Day

My friend Mary Jarlath, born in Dundalk, Ireland, said to me one day in Boston, "The hearts of the Irish are so big because our island is so small." I am convinced that in the huge heart of the Irish, lives generosity, laughter, poetry, and the echoes of their language shared throughout the world. *Go rabh maith agat Mary Jarlath, a carad**.

* In Gaelic: Thank you, Mary Jarlath, my friend.

F. Isabel Campoy

I have dedicated my life to the belief that it is necessary to protect all cultures. How wonderful to conserve your own culture and also enrich yourself with all those around you! Because of this, it is with great pride that I watch my granddaughter Samantha perform dynamic Irish dances as she learns about and appreciates the culture from which they come. While she dances, Samantha becomes one with the music and helps to keep a tradition alive.

Alma Flor Ada

For Diego, Sofia and Beatriz Yaffar Matute,
may music and dance live forever in your hearts.
AFA & FIC

Acknowledgements
Many thanks to Samantha Zubizarreta, excellent Irish dancer and a sensitive person who inspired this book, and her mother, Denise Zubizarreta, for the photographs that contributed to the accuracy of the illustrations.

© This edition:
2006, Santillana USA Publishing Company, Inc.
2105 NW 86th Avenue
Miami, FL 33122
www.santillanausa.com

Text © 2006 Alma Flor Ada and F. Isabel Campoy

Managing Editor: Isabel C. Mendoza
Copyeditor: Eileen Robinson
Art Director: Mónica Candelas

Alfaguara is part of the **Santillana Group**, with offices in the following countries:
ARGENTINA, BOLIVIA, CHILE, COLOMBIA, COSTA RICA, DOMINICAN REPUBLIC, ECUADOR, EL SALVADOR, GUATEMALA, MEXICO, PANAMA, PARAGUAY, PERU, PUERTO RICO, SPAIN, UNITED STATES, URUGUAY, AND VENEZUELA

ISBN: 1-59820-129-8

Published in the United States of America
Printed in Colombia by D'vinni Ltda.

12 11 10 09 08 07 06   1 2 3 4 5 6 7

Library of Congress Cataloging-in-Publication Data

Ada, Alma Flor.
        Celebrate St. Patrick's Day with Samantha and Lola / Alma Flor Ada; F. Isabel Campoy; illustrated by Sandra Lavandeira.
        p. cm. — (Stories to celebrate)
        Summary: Samantha teaches Lola how to do Irish dancing by focusing on one step at a time. Includes information about St. Patrick's Day.
        ISBN 1-59820-129-8
        [1. Saint Patrick's Day—Fiction. 2. Folk dancing, Irish—Fiction. 3. Dance—Fiction. 4. Stories in rhyme.] I. Title: Celebrate Saint Patrick's Day with Samantha and Lola. II. Campoy, F. Isabel. III. Lavandeira, Sandra, ill. IV. Title. V. Series.

PZ8.3.A1835Cel 2006
[E]—dc22   2006000923